MERRY WITH A RANGER

A TEXAS RANGER SECOND CHANCE
CHRISTMAS ROMANCE

TEXAN DEVILS

SOFIA AVES

First Edition

Published by Little Quail Press

ISBN ebook 78-1-922448-89-7

Print 978-1-922448-79-8

CONTENT WARNING

For those who have been following TEXAN DEVILS for a while, Nash came to Rhys Archer as a troubled Texan boy reluctant to return to home soil. His story covers discussions on trauma, recounting of SA, family arguments, a little spanking kink and a few heavier subjects.

TEXAN DEVILS has often been a place where we don't shy away from tough subjects and in honor of Chuck who inspired this series with my nineties obsession of his show, Nash's story stays true to form. If you have triggers, we probably hit them here, but neither I as the author, nor any of my Rangers romanticize any form of trauma or hate speech or actions. Please read safely.

. . .

There's a Ranger out there for you.

CHAPTER 1

N ASH

This assignment was an utter waste of time.

I stared at the waves slapping the shore where the turquoise waves crested into golden sands with pale foam, and pretended I loved frolicking in the fucking sand like everyone else at Love Beach.

Then I cursed myself as a liar inside my own head before I shoved my toes deeper in the sand, praying for a thousand paper cuts to end the monotony of the first four days of my case here. The assignment I begged for with a different workplace and had it handed to me on a sandy platter in a new one.

But I didn't accrue the pain I needed as I linked my arms around my bent knees, letting my jacket hang around my body as I stared out the crashing waves. The cove would've been quieter than this overpopulated spot where tourists were desperate for a glimpse of heat in the midst of winter. A few days from Christmas, it seemed everyone in the destination hot spot tried to frolic in the waves while risking frostbite on occasion—okay, dramatics, but close enough.

But if I limited myself to a quiet area, my head would've been too loud.

Here, at least, I could hate on myself in the over-bearing company of a hundred other cheery people who pretended to cover their own insecurities in brand names and out of season tan lines behind the shade of a giant, unlit Christmas tree that watched us from the boardwalk overlooking the ocean.

Love Beach was so far from Texas in every sense it wasn't funny. A state I never thought I'd return to, and the fact I did miss that patch of dirt imbued with so much sin and blood it wasn't funny that I almost laughed out loud. My heritage of that place disgusted me, but the job Rhys Archer offered me in return for a second chance at sanity on a place called home seemed like a good idea before a bomber blew himself back to hell with my grandfather's name on his lips.

The not so perfect welcome home present.

My teeth ground together as I fixed my gaze on some innocuous point beyond the horizon. The strange things that came to light when I wasn't looking. Or maybe it wasn't funny at all. Instead of seeing the details of what I should be picking out for this case, the only thing I spotted was the one person who could make this day better.

Or so much worse.

Depended on how fucked up my mind was when I reflected on it later.

Because the thing wasn't a thing at all, but a who.

Her. Bonnie Little.

I shouldn't have looked. Not even after ten long years, but I would know her anywhere. Still, I couldn't keep my eyes away from how her long, tanned legs peeked out from beneath the hem of her white sarong that flicked up every now and then to give me a tantalizing glimpse of her ankles.

No jewelry, because she never had been into that. It made buying her presents utter hell.

But I knew those legs. I knew those thighs, her waist, and hips, and everything else above her silky, filmy looking sarong that belonged to her. I didn't need to, but I dragged my eyes up her body anyway, torturing myself further with the girl who left me ten years ago without so much as a single word of goodbye.

The way body curved should've been illegal, enhanced from the last time I saw her. Pale blonde hair hung straight past her shoulders and curled at the ends just enough for man to wrap his finger around and tug before he drove himself slowly insane over that body hidden behind layers of gossamer wrapped around her. The rest of Bonnie Little was hidden beneath a white cardigan she hugged tight around her. But it didn't matter.

I remembered everything about the girl I fell for hard and fast and never recovered from.

What it felt like to kiss those soft, dusky lips that parted temptingly when she sighed. How she liked my thumb digging into her hip when I arched over her, and she submitted beneath me.

Everything.

Before she ran away and left me high and dry, wondering where the fuck she went at the end of our senior year.

The first girl I fell for. The only girl I ever loved.

I found her aqua gaze that matched the sea at the same time as she flicked a wayward glance over her shoulder.

Those lips I could almost feel on mine, despite

being dozens of feet away apart, hitched on a breath, stalling her easy gait. The chattering crowd that had disappeared for me rushed back as her lips silently framed my name before she picked up the material wrapped around legs and whirled away up the beach, away from me.

Nineteen year old Nash would've chased after her. Nineteen year old Nash would have demanded where she went the night she disappeared. The night when she blocked all my calls, and changed her number.

The night she ran.

He would have asked why she broke my heart, and never came back. He would have cared.

Today's Nash tipped his head back as I studied the way she darted away from me, already lost in a pensive memory of Bonnie Little I thought was long locked away behind wall with a plethora of clusterfuck of one-night stands with all the other blonde women who never matched up to the shade of who she should have been in my life. I never could replace her, no matter how hard I tried.

Today's Nash let her go.

I dug my toes into the sand and finally achieved some of those tiny cuts I'd been trying for. Most of them were hardly scratches on the surface of my skin, but it was a start.

The corner of my mouth curled into a sadistic smile.

Bonnie Little could run, but in a town like Love Beach, she couldn't hide. Not for long. She had no chance. Not with me.

Not with an obsession that had been brewing since I last saw her ten years ago. No, this assignment just got a whole lot more interesting. Maybe Love Beach wouldn't be as boring as I expected.

I mentally flipped over the ring that had lived in my pocket since she ran away. Since I never got to give it to the girl who should have been my prom date, but when I went to get her, she wasn't there.

No, Texas could wait.

Sand etched its way along my ass crack despite the three showers I'd taken since I got back from the beach where I spotted my ghost girl who should never have been there in the first place.

The waste of water ingrained in my blood still got to me despite the years I spent outside of Texas. It didn't matter how much of the stuff floated around me or that I was back on the coast, for now. What had been bred into me couldn't be cancelled out on a whim, even for particles as annoying as the tiny grits that seemed determined to mine their way into every unavailable orifice.

But a few grits didn't change my focus as I sifted through files I knew by heart. Photos and names printed in blacks and whites, as well as color covered the resort bed. For the umpteenth time I worked back through the final night of a man's life laid out in front of me, but nothing could change the death of the bomber who knew information about my grandfather he took to the literal grave, albeit in several pieces.

When he blew himself back to hell in County, he left me with a message about the KKK grandmaster I hated who was still attached to my bloodline. I spent a decade away from Texas just to remove myself from the taint of my grandfather's actions, alienating myself from the family who still claimed me despite my pushing them away.

Even with the bomber dead and my grandfather whiling his final years away in respite care, I still scrubbed his sins from my skin daily even though they weren't mine.

Archer, my new boss at the Texas Ranger unit I'd

become attached to when he offered me a position after the FBI failed to provide me with what I needed, had a penchant for manila folders and hard copy files. The resort coffee table and oversized, overstuffed and unsupportive bed was covered with beige cardboard.

The man might be the cream of Texas Rangers down south, but right now I cursed him for his lack of ability to file a digital report like any other human in this century.

Not that Archer was old by any means; I was lucky if he had a decade on me. But from the moment I walked into his office, wary yet keen to accept a second chance and a reason to be back on Texas home soil, I could see the pain etched in his face that haunted the stocky Texas Ranger, his chestnut hair shot with occasional strand of silver.

His office was bare. Not in a rustic sense but stark enough to show he had no personal attachment to anything in it.

But I knew instinctively that it wasn't the things in his office, the tiny little space filled only with a scarred desk as old as the man seated behind it, and a row of equally marred filing cabinets that were the important things in the bigger picture to him. No, that would be the team that sat outside his office.

Those were the critical factors in Rhys Archer's life, and that small fact instinctively told me this was a man I wanted to work for.

Especially when the first thing he did was hand me the one case we both knew I had chased for years, and would never refuse.

My grandfather's eyes stared up at me from the bed in a black-and-white photo. There were color ones of him that existed, sepia even, but I preferred this one. It showed a man in his prime, carrying that hideous white sheath in his unmarked hands. Glowing cheeks that, like so many psychos out there, didn't reflect the insanity festering within.

An insanity I feared might be contained inside me, too.

Not racism. I didn't give a fuck what my grandfather stood, or what sort of twisted moral PR agenda he pushed. That part disgusted me to the worst degree, and I wanted no part of it. No, the part of him that terrified me was that perhaps his darkness somehow passed down to me in some sick gene, and that no matter what I fought for, that part of him would always be a part of me.

That concept terrified me every damn day.

The rest of the local contingent of assholes pictured around him were either dead for the greater majority, or well into their eighties and nineties, living in nursing homes scattered about the state, unable to leave Texas if they wanted to. On the rarer occasion, the pictures weren't as pleasant, and some of my grandfather's cohort stared at the lens with accusing eyes like they expected the technology to steal their souls.

Okay, so for some of them their brand of insanity sat closer to the surface. I didn't glance at my own reflection in the small resort mirror, unwilling to see if my own insanity peeked through just yet.

My phone buzzed beside me. I tapped the screen without looking at it. A picture popped up in my periphery. Flicking the folder closed on my grandfather's face, I glanced across.

Archer: He left you a message.

The single line message accompanied the photograph. I stared at the collection of memorabilia spread across Archer's desk as bile rose into my throat.

Trophies were displayed in one image. My grandfather's personal collection. Proof of his life, his twisted *successes*, delivered courtesy of a dead man. Jewelry, a perfume bottle. Feather fans taken from someone's house he no doubt burned to the ground.

One of his favorite methods. I wanted to retch, but my eye caught on a picture of a pale hair comb just out of focus, similar to a gift I gave to a pretty girl once. But there were more. A diary, pens with men's names engraved on them.

Bowls of crosses, some with burn marks on them. A sickening orgy of evidence, more than I needed.

Everything I needed, beside the witness I'd come to Love Beach to find.

The case I'd tried to get myself assigned to for so many years and now I had it...the magnitude of the sins of my blood floored me. My skin wanted to walk off my bones as I stared at decades of destruction. No man, regardless of his age who had curated this much destruction in his lifetime, should be allowed to recline in a private nursing home with comforts denied by the lives of those he destroyed.

Swearing softly, I closed my phone, flipped all the manila folders over and tossed them into the box beside the bed away from the windows and threw a jacket over the top.

If this was what the assignment was going to be like, then I needed to find the bar. And maybe, my contact.

Two days later I was no closer in discovering the contact I'd been sent to Love Beach to find though I had created an intimate relationship with the bartender. It wasn't remotely close to dinner time, but there was a bottle of Mclellan on the back shelf I had a vested interest in, even if it bankrupted me by the end of the evening.

Throwing on a fresh shirt and grabbing my jacket, I ran my fingers through my hair and grabbed a piece of dragon fruit the housekeeper left in my bowl as an apparent imported Christmas treat. A weird pink and yellow thing with sweet, squishy innards, I'd become accustomed to them.

I headed for the exit, knife in hand ready to peel, when the heavy door shut behind me. I checked belatedly for my keycard—I hadn't locked myself out prematurely, bonus—and flicked the blade out, my mind already running back through the case that stagnated on me days in.

And breathed in a lungful of moonflower.

Bonnie.

That had been the scent she wore the last year we were together. My senses shut down, except maybe one. The single one attuned to her.

The same fingers searching for my key card in my pocket dug a little deeper, confirming the presence of something else there before I ripped my hand free and twisted around, but the hallway stood empty.

She's been here.

Fuck me, we were staying in the same place. The chances of that were... Well. In a place with a holiday floating population that swelled around this week and a limited number of resorts, the chances were high, to be honest. Somehow, I doubted my ex-Texas girl was a local. My heart kickstarted in my chest.

Discarding the desire to write myself off down at the bar for another unproductive evening, I leaned my back against the wall. Uncaring if I had to wait until she finished her dinner and drinks, I work on peeling my fruit no matter how long it took to find her again.

Fifteen minutes later she emerged on her own from a room across the hall from mine. A straw handbag hooked over her arm that looked like a basket decorated with seashells sewn on it. Bonnie wore a white dress that brushed the back of her calves and left a big scoop across her bare back. Risky with night falling, as the chill air picked up outside. Summer it might feel at Love beach year round, right up until the sun set.

The tiny edges of a tattoo peeked out beneath her white dress. I didn't need to see the full picture it represented to know the rest depicted half of a butterfly.

I knew, because the other half was tattooed on my hip. The two together matched to make the butterfly taking full flight. Individually, they perched on their branches, awaiting their other half, unable to fly alone. It was cliche, it was cheap. We were drunk, and teens when we had them done, and for the second time I emptied my bank account for this girl.

But of all the ink I later put on my body, that butterfly was my absolute favorite. No matter what happened between us, I'd never tattoo over it.

Rifling through her handbag and delving arm deep as though she was Mary Poppins, Bonnie didn't see me until it was too late. I finished paring my fruit and put my knife up at the last minute as I stepped into her, my keycard in my hand as though I was heading for my room, not away from it. The deception should have eaten at me, but I was too desperate to have her body contact mine to care, already drunk on the idea of her.

"Heads up, okay, love?" I notched the flat of the blade under her chin, lifting her gaze to meet mine.

And stopped.

Azure eyes found mine and held for the second time in three days, and the floor might as well have dropped out from underneath me. The resort, too.

Christ. It's not meant to be like this.

Or maybe it is.

Somewhere in the crevices of my brain I recognized that I was supposed to be an adult, talk to her, etc., etc., But I was too far gone in her already to care. Her cheeks flushed the prettiest pink, her recognition instant as though my touch and voice was enough to set her off.

She didn't twist away, and I couldn't break my hand from her face, either.

That single point of contact, despite our proximity, stole my breath. Hers too, from the look of it. The sweet scent of moonflower drifted around us with her hair, a golden halo that brushed my shoulders with her momentum. One of her spaghetti straps fell down while she stared up at me.

All I wanted to do was lean and taste her, but that right disappeared the night she ran away from me. From everyone.

Where did you go? Why did you run?

Every question I once screamed at the night sky that never answered back sprinted to the forefront of my mind. But more than that, a flicker of something else darted about in those beautiful turquoise eyes a second before she shut down again, but I saw it.

I knew what to look for with her, because I knew this girl soul deep who was still etched into my bones as well as I knew Texas soil.

Fear.

Bonnie Little was afraid.

Of me.

"The fuck did I do you?"

Ten years apart, and that was the first thing I could think to say to her?

I expected her to run. I expected her to slap me.

Shove me aside, and run away screaming.

But Bonnie Little did none of those things. She shook her chin free of my blade, and stared up at me with those glossy pink lips still parted. Whatever she painted them with had a flicker of glitter in it I wanted to swipe away, get that shit off her. Underneath I could see the dusky color of her mouth underneath, the color I always loved.

But yeah, I lost that right a while back.

We were strangers to each other now.

And all I could think about was that she wasn't afraid of me in this moment.

"What on earth are you eating?"

I huffed at her. "I swear at you, and that's the first thing you say?"

She raised one shoulder, and dropped it. "I mean, it's been a weird day."

"Damn right."

A sweet smile creased her lips, but the expression was gone as fast as it came on with a practiced blankness I hated on her.

"It's dragon fruit." I sliced into the bright flesh to expose its monochromatic insides. "I shouldn't have asked what I did. I had no right. Not anymore." A tightness lodged in my throat I couldn't get past.

Bonnie nibbled on her bottom lip, took half a step back and fixed her dress strap, her fingers playing across her skin in a way that mesmerized me. "I was heading down to the bar before dinner."

"Drowning yourself when the ocean gets too

much?" I didn't know where that came from. It was a stupid line.

"Something like that. Join me?"

I sliced off a piece of the fruit and passed it to her on the flat of the blade. She considered me for a moment before her lips parted. The dragon fruit disappeared as she licked my fingers when I pressed the offering between them, though I knew she wouldn't bite me.

Or maybe she would.

Strangers, remember?

A sharp breath sucked into my lungs. "Little Bonnie. Look at you, all grown up."

Her tongue flicked out to catch a drop of moisture that beaded across the lip gloss, missing my fingertips, though I wish she hadn't.

"Sweet," she acknowledged, stepping away from me and walking away down the hall. She didn't look over her shoulder to check that I followed her, nor did she need to.

She knows I'm all in.

I always was with her.

CHAPTER 2

B ONNIE

Nash Mercer hadn't changed at all. I mean, he'd grown a bit bulkier, added on about three tons of muscle, and there were more tattoos peeking out from his rolled up shirt sleeves and from his collar than when I left him more unmarked back in high school in our senior year. But other than that? He was still the same Texas boy with the sharp eyes who missed nothing and saw enough to land me in a whole lot of trouble.

Which was probably why it was a really good idea to turn tail and run as far away from him as I could right now.

I wasn't sure why I wasn't running, like I did back on the beach. But right now, I didn't want to run. The last time I left Nash Mercer, I regretted it for the next few years until that, like all my other memories, numbed with time.

Or maybe I lied to myself, and nothing really numbed at all.

Not missing prom with the boy I hoped I might marry one day, have the whole picket fence, and all. Except in our world it was more likely a mansion than a picket fence. Or it was supposed to be. Two rich kids, neither of us from the wrong side of the track, who fell in love one summer and never got our happily ever after.

Maybe that's why it didn't work. Back then we had everything going for us. Before the world knew who his family was, and before my life...disintegrated.

One night, and everything changed. A simple dream of attending college together, getting married and living a stress-free life. What a joke. Nothing was stress free, but then kids think that way. At least, some do, for a short time. My over-entitled childhood was stripped away alongside my happy dreams that left me as cold and lifeless as the dim, ground floor resort corridor I traversed before Nash caught me up.

He walked along behind me for two floors, neither of us speaking. Ten years of non-history stood between us. I didn't know who he'd become in that time, and I couldn't tell him anything about myself. Whatever I said tonight would be a lie on top of more lies.

My eyes closed briefly as his fingers grazed my elbow, the flat of his blade still slightly sticky with the dragon fruit's pale pips from the sweet slice he offered me before.

And I took it straight from the knife that he slid between my lips, eating it with my eyes locked on him. *This boy makes me as mad for him as I was back then.* Before everything shattered. Our dreams, my sanity. My...everything.

But Nash Mercer wasn't a boy anymore. Hadn't been one for a long time, by the looks of him.

He flashed me a sideways glance without a smile, eyes dark, his face cast in sharp relief beneath the resort's bright overhead lighting that left him half brightly lit, the other half of him lost in shadows of his own making.

I was wrong. He had changed. I didn't know him anymore than I knew myself.

"What's Little Bonnie drinking tonight?"

He held the door to the bar for me, taking us from the bright white and blue downstairs halls to the darker lit, wooden based interior of the dining and bar area. I studied the giant Christmas tree—a real one, not plastic—trimmed within an inch of its life with crystalline snowflakes, hand painted, glittery baubles and perfectly tied burgundy velvet bows, lit from within with tiny, muted lights.

They glow on a strange frequency, not quite on and off, more a three on, one off, two on...it was an odd pattern. I stood beside him in the doorway, transfixed as I try to figure it out.

"I can see your brain working, love," Nash's low voice brushed my ear as he tucked my hair back. Rough knuckles grazed my skin, eliciting a shiver I wanted to hide from him. *Dangerous*. My mind screamed at me, but it was too late. I tried to twist away, but my feet rooted to the spot as his heat enveloped me, the door closing gently at our backs. "It's always been one of my favorite parts of you."

I forgot what he was talking about, and took a moment too long to catch up as he folded his body around mine like he was always supposed to be there. "Not that I ever got to use it." I clamped my mouth shut. "Sorry, that was stupid."

"Nothing about you is stupid." The hand that touched me glided lower to settle at the small of my back. "Drink?" That he ignored my faux pas and didn't ask questions was a relief. Like we'd fallen back into old patterns.

I closed my eyes and let him propel me gently to the bar. *This is Nash. I can trust him.* But also, this was *Nash.* I couldn't trust him because of who he was. Where he comes from.

Home.

I never got over leaving Texas. I'd also never been back. My last request that night was to push the driver to go back past the school, past the kids all gathered out the front for prom. My first mistake. My last, there. Because Nash stood apart from everyone, his brow furrowed, phone in his hand. Mine would have been pinging, back at home, but I wasn't that girl anymore, and she couldn't answer him.

His face raised, worry written all over the youth in him that died that day.

And some other part of me that I managed to salvage, that I held on to tight...that part died that night with him, too.

"What are you having, ma'am?" the bartender asked politely in that sort of tone that said it wasn't the first time he'd asked.

Nash's fingers flexed my back, and his sharp, indrawn breath said he was about to rescue me with an order he pulled out of his ass, as always. But I had my big girl panties on tonight, and I could save myself.

"Um, that one. Please." I poked blindly at a drink name I didn't recognize, and pasted a fake smile on my face.

My big girl panties were a silky white thong that matched the dress, and they were slipping.

"Doing good," Nash muttered under his breath, rubbing my lower back in a way that drew shocks along my spine. Literally no one had touched me that way, not since...

Well, him.

I swallowed hard, certain the bartender heard, but Nash's voice stayed low enough for only me to hear, apparently. I flashed him a grateful, if strained smile, and said the first thing that tumbled from my lips. "What have you been doing with yourself?"

"Professional surfer." His mouth tightened a fraction, enough for me to read the lie in him without checking him for tan lines...and I already did that back on the beach in a half second glance.

The only tan line Nash Mercer sported was one

involving a shirt and tie outlined over his lying heart.

Don't know him anymore, my butt.

At least our deceptions matched.

"Surfer. Right." My words had a flatness I couldn't erase.

"Yeah." He swallowed, taking the whiskey the bartender poured for him, a double shot, and downed it in one. We had the same goal tonight, apparently. "You?"

"Elementary school teacher."

I took perverse pleasure in watching him choke on the overpriced alcohol and smiled innocuously as my own blue drink arrived, topped with an excess of cream, cherries, something that looked like sand from the beach, and a lackluster umbrella that refused to stay up.

From the look on his face, Nash knew just how that felt.

"Yeah?" He thumped his chest in an effort to breathe, his touch at my back wavering for just a second before he was back. His eyes zeroed in on me. "Happy with that career choice, Bonnie?"

The bartender made an excellent decision in heading up the other end of the bar to clean sparkling glasses.

I nodded and sipped my drink, failing in my attempt not to screw up my face with the excess of sugar. "Holy fuck," I whispered, loud enough for the bartender to snort up the other end of the bar, polishing away with an ardency I was sure the hotel manager would have adored.

Nash leaned in. "Bullshit tastes fine in that filthy mouth, huh, Teach?" His fingers trailed along my side as he sighed. "You know, I promised myself I was gonna try to take it slow with you, not get involved, all the right things, but..." He swiveled me around to face him in full, and there was no disguising the unslaked need in his eyes that reflected Christmas lights in all the wrong ways I suddenly craved. "You're making that damn hard."

I licked the obscenely sweet liquor off my lips. "My tongue is numb," I muttered.

He huffed, wrapping an arm around my waist and pulling me in close. "Got dinner plans, love?"

"My f– folks." My tongue played hardball, but I got the F word out, eventually.

Nash's face closed. "Your daddy's here? I wouldn't mind having a word with him."

My hair whipped my face, horror settling as I realized what he meant, but his attention already shifted. "No, that's a really bad idea–" Suddenly I was a seventeen year old girl with her life back in tatters, her arms around her legs trapped in a tatty t-shirt and a pair of ripped jeans that felt too tight and too big all at once while the rest of her class was dressed to the nines and her date grew angrier, like he did right now. "Nash, no–"

He turned on the spot, right as the door to the dining room opened, and my mother walked in, dressed in the same pants suit she'd worn to dinner every night this week. Her hair was done in the same way it had been when I was a girl. Nothing changed about her but for the vague expression on her face when she looked past me like I wasn't even there.

By now I was used to it. Nash, on the other hand, hadn't experienced my mother's mood swings where I spent the past decade growing used to them, *after*. They were my fault, after all.

My father, however—his sharp gaze lit on Nash and locked there.

"Good to see you again, son." His tone implied anything but as he glanced at me for confirmation that he hadn't started his own bout of hallucinations.

I nodded, detaching myself gently but there was no need. Nash's hand lay limp at his side.

"Daddy. You remember Nash?"

The two men stared at each other, both as stiff as

dead men reawakening after an eternity beneath unturned Texas soil.

"Of course." My mother, so used to springing into action when needed though the brain cells long ceased to actually function, did so on demand as an automaton.

The shock of her Stepford wife-ish Mom-bot on his arm, her cheek upturned for her kiss, her blank expression, jolted Nash out of his stupor. A glance at me, and he leaned down to kiss her, murmuring soft, kind words to her ear though his flapping hand behind him gave away his freaked out reaction to the surreality of the situation.

I was the girl he should have taken to prom.

The girl who disappeared.

I had no idea what they all said afterward, but I read the hurt, the panic, the anger in his face that night. The abandonment.

I should never have asked the driver to take me past the school.

Daddy still didn't know about that. The detective took one look at my tear-stained face afterward, cursed enough to provide me with an extended vocabulary, and took me straight to the station like we should have agreed to much earlier.

That was the last time I saw Nash Mercer until that afternoon at Love Beach a few days ago.

I didn't know if fate brought us back together. I didn't know if he could accept the person I'd become, but I did know one thing.

Tonight's dinner would be an utter shitfight—*if* he survived the questioning my father put him through afterwards.

I managed a faint smile, less than reassuring and all the things he needed as my broken mother retracted and headed toward the table in the corner we occupied all week because it appeared to be the only one in the room she could find.

My father continued to stare at Nash. After a while he held out a hand for the boy who never got a chance to say goodbye to follow the woman he refused to abandon when another might have.

Nash looked down at me, his eyes fathomless. Unchecked fury swirled in their depths. Tonight, I'd have questions to answer about our shared past, even though he didn't know that last part yet.

I didn't glance at Daddy, but I did keep my hand laced through Nash's as I followed him to our table.

Shitfight was absolutely the right term.

One of those words I learned from the detective that night.

CHAPTER 3

N ASH

Dinner was torture. Silent, pure death.

Thankfully, Bonnie chose the seat next to me, though her shell of a mother perched on my other side so I got the full blast of her father's interrogative stare across the table. That was okay. I understood him. Bonnie's mom, on the other hand...

Well, I understood her, too.

All too well.

I spent years in the FBI talking to traumatized women in various stages of recovery, trying to help them grasp details they barely remembered, or readying them for the stand in the hope that on the day they would be the performing monkey we all needed in order to put the sons of bitches who created the trauma away for a long, long time.

Occasionally, it worked.

Often, our processes created more damage than was there when we started. I hated it. Pinned between the two women, Bonnie with her innocent doe eyes staring beseechingly at me, and Mrs Little with her blank face that recognized no one, made the first steps to purgatory I earned myself dozens of times over for all the above reasons. Not that her mom seemed to know her husband or her child when Bonnie spoke to her across me, but somewhere in there Sarah Little recognized one thing: this conversation had to go on, and she was expected to be a part of it.

She played her role, just like everyone else at the table. Hers just came out a little more obvious, and stilted.

My heart ached for all of them, including the angry, protective father and husband seated across from me who seemed intent on ashing me with a single glare.

Unfortunately for him, that hadn't happened for me yet.

The moment my knife sat next to my fork across

my plate he slapped the table decisively, jerking Bonnie out of her stupor where she shredded her paper napkin systematically into her lap beside me.

"Right. Nash and I need a chat on the balcony with a nice glass of that whiskey you were killing before we came in. Or three." His eyes warned me I wasn't taking Bonnie back to my room tonight, or any other night.

A twenty-seven year old woman who was fast on her way to becoming a mirror of her empty shell of a mother, in all respects. My spine stiffened, but I knew this conversation was coming the moment I saw him. To be honest, as much as I knew it would sting, my curiosity won out fair and square. Bonnie and I spent ten minutes at the bar earlier, lying our asses off to each other.

This man would slap me in the face with the truth for my own good and tell me to thank him for it.

I would, with a few hand selections of my own right back.

"Yes, sir." I rose, dragging my fingertips along Bonnie's upper arm in full sight—nothing hidden here—anticipating her reaction.

She didn't disappoint.

Her shiver was a full body effort that left the

scant remains of her napkin in confetti. A large part of me needed her beneath my weight the next time she did that, but first I had to deal with a different sort of threat who seemed to have no idea of the damage he did to his daughter.

"Two, please." My knuckles rapped the bar top lightly at the back of the room. The bartender didn't have a big job tonight; either everyone ate out, or the resort wasn't doing its job well over Christmas. "Event in town tonight?"

"Yacht party at the marina. You know rich kids. Plus the night markets on the boardwalk." His knowing gaze told me he recognized my ilk.

I nodded back and didn't ask him to throw his wisdom my way. Something told me I'd regret it. Hands filled with two generous fingers each to match the tip from earlier, I winked at Bonnie as she escorted her mother back toward the rooms.

Her lips sliding between whitened teeth, her gaze darted to the balcony and back. Hesitating for a second, she parked her mother in stasis near the door and the barman, and dashed back to me.

"I won't be that long." I searched her eyes, frowning.

"I never got to tell you anything." Her eyes glazed with more salt than the ocean beyond the closed doors, though a rushing far louder than the sea filled my ears the moment she started to speak. "I– there isn't enough time. Please find me afterward. I need to apologize."

"Bonnie, there's nothing—"

She shook her head, vehement. "You can't say that, Nash." One tear jeweled her lashes like a glistening Christmas bauble. "You don't *know*."

I swallowed hard. "You should have stayed." I backed up a step, and another as she mouthed two words that ripped me apart inside. The kid I'd been looking for her that night, and the man I'd been five minutes ago, still clinging to a futile specter of hope, died a little.

I couldn't.

Nothing else.

Turning my back to Bonnie, I paraded across the dining room floor to find her father outside and prayed I'd go numb in the night's ocean freezing air before he said anything else that stung.

Maybe I wasn't half as prepared as I thought.

Kicking the sliding door gently shut behind me, I walked along the balcony where the wind picked up around the side of the building in a veritable gale. Naturally, that's where her father stood, his hands latched around the railing as though it would keep his bulk that was in no way threatened in blowing away on solid ground.

I coughed discreetly and passed over the glass. "Sir."

He took the glass without looking. There was a measure of trust I didn't expect.

"I know who you are, Mercer." He stared across the sand, up the long beach where white caps flickered further out to sea while the waves themselves were eaten by the darkness.

"I missed her that night." My voice stayed quiet, almost lost in the wind.

Almost.

He sighed. "We both did. She ever tell you?"

I shook my head, though he couldn't see the motion, and joined him at the railing, both our drinks untouched. "I spoke to her this afternoon for the first time in ten years, sir. Real gut punch. Thought...thought I was over her, you know. The disappearance. Don't know if you understood what happened after. The town was in an uproar. You all ran off. No one knew what happened. Speculation. Lies, rumors...the works. Her name..." I shook my head and dipped my neck between my shoulders, stretching muscles that were never right after that night, but they weren't ready to give, yet. "I tried to quell them but I gotta admit even I struggled with that. After a while I got silent, too. Wondered where she'd gone. What happened to make you all run."

The words fell out and I cursed myself internally for being so verbose. The silent dinner hit me in all the right/wrong places. But as I glanced sideways at the father staring into the darkness, I knew I wasn't the only one affected that way. He just showed his fears, his stress differently.

Grant Little didn't move. Not a word or a breath escaped him, though he didn't hold back on purpose, turn purple or swell like an over puffed bullfrog. Nothing. That was a skill under duress. A learned trait. Or maybe this man endured so much that he'd mastered the art of stillness. An acquired skill.

"We were...required to leave." He spoke to the night, the wind whipping his words away the moment he spoke, but my trained ear picked up each one, already knowing the bullshit story he was about to spin for me. "Headed north, got out of town after my wife's first turn. Couldn't stay around after that. Too much for her," he said gruffly, as though emotion caught up with him.

Or the lies of ten years eating away a conscience never meant for it.

I turned my glass in my hands and took a deep drink. Letting the pain then the smoothness roll through me, and found the best words I could, planted them on target.

"I used to respect you, sir." I stood side on so I looked him straight in the eyes, if only he'd face me but of course after that, he couldn't. "That was more bullshit than a rodeo clown deals with on a Saturday night."

Grant huffed at the air. What might have been a laugh died in his chest cavity. "Quick wit," he muttered. "She'll like that."

My throat tightened. *This is why investigations and personal life should never clash.* "I wasn't here for her," I murmured.

"No. You're FBI now, aren't you? S'pose you can't tell me the case you're working."

My eyebrows shot up, a response I couldn't curb if I wanted to. "Someone kept up with the local news," I observed, finishing my glass in one.

He eyed me, finally. "They teach you to drink like that, too, son?"

I snorted. "I started drinking the day I went to your house, found the door unlocked, and your daughter's phone on the bed, my messages and calls unread and unanswered. I woulda called the cops, but they were swarming all over your front lawn. You're the reason I chose that career, Mister Little."

He winced. "Lawson. It's Lawson, now. We... changed it. To protect my wife."

"Lawson." I sucked in that extra piece of bullshit and filed it away for later. Archer's cynicism was rubbing off on me. "I tried to open a file on Bonnie, but that got closed on me, time and again." I met his gaze, refused to back down.

You wouldn't have anything to do with that, would you? With your money and friends and power?

I didn't believe a word about everything being to protect the mother who took a turn. Sure, she was damaged as hell from trauma. I got that, loud and clear, and it was horrible. Bonnie wasn't the same, either. Something happened to them, but no one talked to me, then or now.

"So you could look for her?" he challenged.

"So I could stop what the fuck ever happened to her from happening to any other girl," I fired back. Swiping a hand through my hair, I shook my head. "It doesn't matter, honestly. What happened, happened. I can't stop that. Hell, my family is a clusterfuck of its own." He stiffened, but I barraged on. "I only just got back to Texas after walking away for years. Finally got the case I wanted after all this time. Because the FBI wouldn't give it to me."

He frowned. "You're not FBI anymore?"

I shake my head. "Texas Ranger, brand spanking new." There was no keeping the pride out of my voice. I mightn't have been sure when Archer first called me, but I damn well was by the time I walked out of his office, hat and badge in hand.

Grant stared at me. For the first time the edge of his mouth smoothed out of the permanent frown it had lived in since he entered the dining room. "Not a bad career choice after all. What's the case you've been chasing all this time, then?"

Night air and sea salt filled my lungs on an inhale that made me wish I was back inside with Bonnie in my arms.

If she'd let me touch her.

"Taking my grandfather and his cohort out of their comfortable retirement homes and putting them into solitary where they fucking well belong. Lot of lives they damaged in their reign of terror. Apparently one of my key witnesses is a local for the season."

Turning away from the horror on his face, I let the obsession that burned within my chest for too long as an ember take full root. *Consume me.*

"Thanks for the chat, Mister Lawson."

I turned away from the man I could have called *dad* if all the stars aligned and headed back to find his daughter, if she'd see me. If not, I had work to do. Sleep was meaningless after all these years.

I'd learned to live on little of it.

CHAPTER 4

BONNIE

Snores emanated from the unit next door that we rented. I locked the door between us, keeping my father out as I knew he'd want to talk—or rant—after he and Nash parted ways. Whatever their beef, I wanted no part of it. Those years were so long ago and yet still yesterday but the dread of it all followed me like I couldn't step away from it. From them.

Him.

And yet Nash was here. I wanted him near me, holding my hand like he used to, and asking me to dance with hope in his eyes and a tremor in his fingers.

But the Nash I met again forged his own path and didn't have time for hope or simple things like dancing. And I was simply the forgotten girl whose childhood fell away before she became an adult who didn't get to play with simple dreams and things like hope any more.

Swallowing back the way of blackness that threatened to push me to the carpet, weighing me down. I forced one foot in front of the other, glancing back at the interlocking doorway that connected mine and my parent's room, knowing they would be furious if I left, but I hadn't been a teenager for a long, long time.

Nor, in all those years, had I claimed any sense of freedom or self at all.

Regardless, I still slipped out the door of my room with my keycard clutched in hand like I was sixteen, checking the hallway in both directions and ignoring the camera at the end of the corridor that wasn't recording anyway.

It couldn't be, when I was around. They made sure of it.

A familiar pressure built in my throat as I closed the door gently to an empty hallway. I made it all the way to the end, so ready to taste outside air, and walked straight into a familiar checked shirt and an unforgiving chest that most definitely wasn't that hard last time I had intimate contact with it.

"Your father is right behind me." Nash's brusque voice sent a riot of sensation along my skin in every direction, sweeping away the pressure and replacing it with something different. A shot of adrenaline I hadn't felt in far too long. His hands directed my body to turn, and I did, back the way I came. "Move it, Bonnie, or we lose any chance we have."

I quick-stepped it halfway up the hall, unsure if he was directing me back to my room or his, when his arm braced the wall before me and suddenly I shifted sideways into a stairwell I previously ignored.

"Fire escape." His lips brushed my ear. "Keep moving. Next landing, then stop. Okay?'

I nodded, my lips as unable to move as they did on that truly hideous cocktail earlier, or over that stilted dinner that killed every fraction of freedom Nash and I displayed before with our lies.

But this felt nothing like either of those moments.

A breath later and the fire escape door shut gently behind him. Nash's feet moved soundlessly to where I stood on the next landing under the cement stairs below. His fingers flicked sideways and I started on the next flight downward, halting in the shadows when he held up a hand.

My feet stalled. I froze as he took the next stair, stopping just above me, waiting.

Nothing. The door didn't open, nor did my father seem to know where Nash disappeared to, or that I was with him.

I opened my mouth, but his hand pressed to my stomach in a light touch. Light, but a warning all the same. *Count*, he mouthed to me.

I bit my lip, watching him, and counted in my head.

One Mississippi, two Mississippi...

By the time I got to five, Nash's body heat met mine on the same step. He wasn't bulky by any means, but his sort of muscle was still the solid sort, the type of man who'd be impossible to outrun.

This was Nash Mercer. If ever there was someone in this world to be terrified of, it was him. Because he knew me, and I couldn't hide from him.

But I wasn't terrified. Much.

My fingers brushed his collar, reaching up to find a few days' growth on his chin. "I like you like this," I mumbled into the darkness, unable to see his full face.

His hands braced against the wall behind me over my head. "I was gonna take you outside. Wanted to walk somewhere. But it's kinda freezing."

"I like freezing." My head tipped back as I searched for his eyes, twin pinpoints of onyx in the roiling shadows he wore like a cloak. "Nash, what did he tell you—"

"Nothing."

"Oh." I swallowed, both relieved and back to being a little terrified at once.

"It's your story to tell, Bonnie Lawson."

Shit. My language really was going to get me into trouble with this man as I mouthed the word. His fingertips followed, tracing the movement of my lips. "What if I don't want to tell you?" *What if I can't?*

He shrugged. "Then you don't tell me. It's been a long damn time, Bonnie. Trust is built. Earned."

I could see the pain it cost him to admit that, but this wasn't just his story. "I broke that trust when we left. When I left."

"You were seventeen. There wasn't exactly a lot of choice. You were at school, Bonnie. A kid. We all were."

"I had to grow up pretty fast." I played with his buttons on his shirt, accidentally popped the top one open.

"Yeah?" His breath came fast, a little less regular against my cheek. "You sure as hell look grown up to me now, Bonnie."

"I don't know if I am," I whispered back. "It's been a long time living like this, place to place, never stopping or settling..." I squeezed my eyes shut, but hot tears escaped anyway.

"Christ." One hand dropped to skate along my back, forcing its way between me and the wall. "You've been stuck like this for all that time..." The penny drops hard and fast. I didn't need to look at him to see it. "Fuck me. You're my—" He coughed into my hair, and the hand on my back dug into my skin beneath my dress. "You're in WITSEC, aren't you? Witness protection. Did your father Marshal up or something?" His dry humor fell endlessly.

I didn't bother to respond. "They're always watching. Just not...like you think." I leaned my forehead on his shirt and breathed in. Salt, whiskey and caramel. My cheek rested against his chest unbidden, and he let me steal a moment's comfort, still braced over me while his heart raced. "You're not a surfer, are you?"

He laughed, a hollow sound that rang around us. "Before this all gets shot to shit and I can pretend for half a second that I'm gonna have that picket fence with the girl I dreamed about for the last ten years, you gonna let me kiss you, Bonnie Little?"

He said Little. Not Lawson.

A sob tried to break free from my lips, but it seemed like Nash was done asking permission. His mouth found mine, his kiss as smooth as that caramel I scented on him before. Deft fingers wound through my hair, tilting my head to the angle he needed. I managed a long inhale on instinct before an all-male noise rose in his throat and his kiss changed into something darker, harder.

Whatever sort of picket fence Nash Mercer wanted, I was here for it.

His other hand banded around my waist, pushing me back into the wall. One knee speared between my legs, then the other, pushing my legs open to the limits of my dress. He cursed, freeing my waist to grip the fabric and yank upward. One hand settled on my thigh in a possessive grip that left me arching into him and his mouth returned to mine in fervor.

Hips grinding roughly into me, his tongue delving deep, Nash engulfed me until I swore nothing remained of Bonnie Little except an echo of a girl who craved a man she couldn't have.

But he was here right now, and I wanted him like I'd never been allowed to have anyone.

Linking one thigh over his hip, I levered myself up, clawing his neck as I kissed him back, sloppy and frantic and with no idea what the hell I was supposed to be doing.

"Damn, girl. You taste just like you used to. Texas summers and stolen midnights together. You remember those? I used to come and get you, drive you to the lookout and–" He pressed his body to mine in a slow grind I felt to my bones.

"Fuck," we whispered together.

"Girl, that mouth." His curled up in a slow smile that echoed to the tips of my toes. "Gonna get you in so much trouble."

"I remember everything." I tried to ignore the way my body lit up the closer he pressed until everything important evacuated from my body. *Air, blood, thoughts.* "Nash, I'm– I don't know what I'm doing."

He froze at my confession, those strong hands releasing me to press back over my head as his body arced against mine. "Say that again, love," he demanded.

But neither the words nor my mouth would cooperate. I shook my head, sucking my bottom lip into my mouth.

His gaze zeroed in on the movement when it popped back out. "Are you telling me—"

We teased and played with each other back in the day, back in Texas, but we were young, and he never pushed me for anything he didn't think I was ready for. Ever the gentleman, Nash Mercer, so before him, I remained a virgin.

I'd always wished he hadn't been quite so gentlemanly after all.

I blinked as his whole body backed off, and it became abundantly clear what he thought. "Oh, no. I'm not...you know. Innocent, or anything." I looked down, but that just left me staring at the straining bulge in his jeans. *Fail.* So I studied his rumpled shirt instead. "No, I mean, I've done— I've— I just don't know anything. That's all," I finished awkwardly.

One moment I was studying his shirt, the next I found myself in freefall in his eyes.

"Are you telling me that after ten long damn years of wishing I'd been the one to be with you back then, there's a chance I can still give you some of your firsts?" His frown was offset by the way his eyes searched my face, seeking answers I didn't want to give but needed to answer all the same.

I nodded, worrying my lip until it ached. "Mhmm."

Nash settled his body against mine, pressing in the damning rhythm again. "Words, love," he murmured, his voice a seduction all on its own.

"Yes, Nash. Anything I've got left to give is yours."

His mouth crashed down on mine, and ten years dissipated in a breath. He kissed me until my head swam with the scent of him, the warmth of his arms folding me into his chest twisted into the fabric of me that no one had ever been able to change no matter how caged and limited my life had been, all these years.

Nash snapped those tethers in seconds. Sliding his hands over my hips, he pulled me hard up against him, his thick erection hitting all the right spots as his body pressed into me relentlessly. I arched back, learning what he liked, a strangled whimper sliding between my lips to seek his mouth—

He pulled back with a groan and drew me down the stairs.

"What's going on?" I shook my head, dizzy from the change in tempo, swaying where I stood.

Nash cursed softly and drew me back to his side, pressing a kiss to my hair. "If I get to have some of your firsts, Bonnie, then I want one I never did back then."

"What's that?"

Letting him tuck me unto his side, I clung to him

as we traversed the final stairs to the ground floor. He pushed open the door to the outside without setting off alarms, though somehow with him, I wasn't surprised.

"I'm taking you to the Christmas markets. And after that abysmal damn dinner, I'm buying you ice cream." He yanked off his jacket and tucked it around me, covering me in the scent of him, and hauled me outside.

CHAPTER 5

NASH

I was buying her ice cream. I didn't care if it was penguin weather outside. The temperate air of Love Beach turned icy as the wind picked up off the ocean and swept in like Santa Claus decided to bring the ice caps along for the ride this silly season.

With a day left to go before Christmas Eve hit—damn, I lost track of days hauling my ass across the country, then finding Bonnie—the entire population of the small town was out at the beachside night markets. No wonder the resort emptied of its floating population for the evening.

Vendors sold everything from gingerbread spiced lattes that scented the salty, sticky air with cloves and ginger and cinnamon. Giant Yorkshire puddings were offered by another shop. Hand blown, glass ornaments swung gently from all angels of a wooden hut, despite the wind, their tinkle audible where they dangled on long ribbons. Glowing neon reindeer, waving Santas, and other assorted Christmas light paraphernalia covered every inch of sand and boardwalk as far as I could see.

Bonnie walked beside me, her hand wrapped around mine as she licked a vanilla—of all things—ice cream like it was the best treat she'd ever had.

I eyed her, willing myself not to get hard or grow too envious of the attention she gave a melting cone that was my idea to get her in the first place, and finally put words into action. "When was the last time you ordered dessert?"

Her eyes slid sideways, and I knew the answer to that before she said a word. "Daddy doesn't really allow it. Not unless it's one of those little biscuits that comes with coffee."

"Mhmm." The sound I made in the back of my throat came out rude, but Grant Lawson wasn't the respectful man I remembered from my youth.

Back then, I'd been afraid of him. I needed his approval to date his daughter, and I wanted to be worthy of them both. Now, he seemed to be afraid of me. The tables had turned. For some stupid reason, I preferred the status quo the other way around.

"Don't be like that." She finished the damn ice cream and licked her fingers, subjecting me to a fresh form of torture. "He does the best he can."

"How's that?" I didn't look sideways at her, and managed to keep my hand loose around hers.

Bonnie halted for a second but when I didn't stop with her she hurried to catch up, her pinkie still getting a suction clean in her mouth. "He's trying. You know, with Mom—"

I growled, frightening several market goers who gave us a wide berth as I spun on my heel, yanked the fingers out of her mouth and drew her close. "You can stop the bullshit about your mother. Yes, I get she's traumatized. It's horrible, Bonnie. But I've seen it enough to know that doesn't 'just happen', okay? Stop lying to me, and tell me what happened to you. Or don't. But don't expect me to believe the bullshit you've been spinning to the rest of the world and getting by on for the last ten years." I didn't step back, and I didn't give her space, knowing I pushed her way too hard.

Bonnie nodded, holding my gaze. "Okay. That seems fair."

The fuck?

"It does?" I let out a measured breath. "Bonnie..."

She held up a hand. "You gave me a choice. I'm taking the latter, for now. Maybe later, when we aren't...here, alright?" Her voice dropped an octave, begging me not to push her in public.

"Am I that much of an asshole you think I'll do that to you?" My mouth softened, and all I wanted to do was kiss her until the sun rose on Christmas morning.

Not practical, but then, closet romantics like me rarely were.

"No, I don't think that. Come on. I want to see the tree." She pointed shyly along the boardwalk to where a large tree was surrounded by glowing sheep, angels and what looked like dangling stars that wobbled only a little precariously in the high winds.

"You haven't been out to look at any of this?" I squeezed her hand gently. "Not prying. I genuinely want to know what you've done and haven't." And I was prying. But in the sweetest, least assholic way I could think to do.

"Nope." That was all the answer she'd give me, towing me along behind her as she wove her way through the small crowd that seemed to grow with the late hour, rather than disperse.

"Alright." I shrugged, following her until she burst out into a clear area beside the giant tree that seemed to go on forever, even to a guy my height. "Hey." I wound my arms around her from behind, nuzzling into her hair. "We need a signal for every time something happens to you that you like and that's a first, okay?"

She laughed softly, scratching her nails lightly over the back of my hands. "What if I don't like it?"

I bit back a groan as her nails dug in a little, and I imagined her doing that to my back. "Then you gotta tell me so I learn you, okay? That's what trust builds on."

"I think we already have a bit of that." She breathed in, and pressed her body back into mine. "This. Now."

"Now?" I nuzzled into her hair, kissing the side of her throat as she made muffled squeaking sounds that drowned out the rest of the crowd altogether for me.

"Yes," she breathed, digging her nails right into my hands.

I pressed mine to her stomach, pulling her back into me. "This too?" I licked the slope of her neck and swore she fucking melted into me.

"Yeah, that," she said faintly, tipping her head

back to stare up the tree and the stars waving above us. "I don't want to leave here."

It was a child's wish, and for a moment her simple prayer stalled me. That's how cloistered her life had been. While I'd been screwing around with the FBI, making a career I was proud of, progressing enough that Archer knew my name and called when he had a vacancy, giving me a job in his Texas Ranger unit, and not buying myself the dog and house I promised I always would, she'd been...

What, exactly?

Living week to week in apartments with her mother and father watching over her shoulder. Living off their money and not having a life of her own. *Elementary school teacher my ass.* The stupidest thing about it all was that the girl in my arms had—has—the brains to do anything she wanted. She should have been prom queen. Valedictorian.

The girl I should have proposed to, after prom.

Instead I lost her, and she lost herself along the way, it seemed.

"Come back with me." I pulled her around roughly to face me. Her lips opened in a frozen 'o' as though she couldn't make the sound, but her pretty mouth framed it anyway. "Come back to Texas with me. I've got a rental place, and a new job. Needed the change, and it was time. I promised myself I'd buy a house, and a dog, but those things haven't happened for me yet. It's like I was...waiting for something." I swallowed my own wish. "Someone."

She stared at me, those blonde curls moving side to side, a negative on her lips, right there. I didn't want to hear it, and kissed her just to keep the pretense up for another minute. Slim arms wound around my neck as she pressed her body to mine.

"So...lots of surfing in Texas, huh?" She looked up at me through her lashes, calling me out on my bullshit point blank for the second time, unafraid.

This woman.

I grinned against her mouth. "Bit of a new thing. Had some things to wrap up here. But you're a pretty distraction." A lie. She was so much more than a distraction. At least, I thought she was from the indications her father gave me. But that was tomorrow Nash's problem.

"I can't go home."

Four words that ruined a future for us both. Just as I thought I had this life thing all figured out, fate sent me a moonflower scented curveball like her.

"Yeah? Where would home be?" I tucked her hair behind her ear. "What would it look like?" I pleaded with her, begging to know what she wanted. *Desperate.*

She shrugged. "I don't know. It's not something I can ever have so I never thought about it."

"There has to be something you want," I persisted, knowing I pushed her for all the selfish reasons now. I had committed to Archer's unit. Walking away was career suicide. But she was worth more than any career. Always had been.

"What I want." Her brow dipped low as she turned the idea over like it was a novelty. Maybe to her, it was exactly that. "I think...that white picket fence would be pretty. I don't care where, as long as it's with you." She leaned down after dropping that bomb of a pronouncement, and snuggled into my chest. "Oh, aneeeog."

"Huh, love?" I tapped the back of her head, then wound my fingers through her hair because it was too damn soft to avoid touching. "Say that last bit again." I was surprised that words came out at all.

She left me damn on breathless being so damn so close, saying all the things I wanted to hear more than anything in the world.

"And the dog. It's a good idea." She beamed up at me, and I saw what she did reflected in her eyes—an untouchable dream. A fairytale that wasn't real.

She'd stay in this moment with me, say what she really wanted because no part of her ever believed that it would come true.

Because that had been her shitty world since I saw her last.

Caged. Bound.

I needed to burn something or ash someone.

Instead, I gathered her close before the giant Christmas tree, the one with all the fake lights, and dangling stars, and dared to make a wish of my own. "What sort of dog would we have?"

"I don't know. I've never been allowed to have one of those, either. But I like big ones. The sort you can cuddle, but that you know will eat anyone who comes in that isn't supposed to be there."

I stared hard at the top of her head. "Aren't you full of the best sort of surprises, Bonnie Little?"

"Shh." She peeked up from her cozy place against my chest. "I'm not supposed to use—"

"Yeah, I know. Lawson and all." I sigh. "Don't worry, love. I won't get you hurt, okay? I get how it works."

The fact no one had come to rip her off me yet surprised me, but then maybe Archer put in a call. The man seemed to have an invisible and unending stream of clout that far exceeded his geographical territory.

She shrugged. "No one ever comes to see me. I just know they're there. It's scary. I hate it." She shivered in my arms, and I wrapped her tighter.

"You want to head back?" Another answer I knew. Maybe she was right about the trust thing. About knowing each other.

"Not yet." Decisive. Saying, not asking. We'd definitely established a baseline of trust even if it was forged on a decade of fairytale worthy hopes and dreams.

"Okay. Whatever you need, love." I turned her back around to stare up the tree.

We didn't move for an age. Not when the small choir of school aged children came by to serenade us, or the herd of baby reindeer paraded by, though she made cooing sounds. Or when a string quartet played a few carols before moving along.

Only when everyone started to pack up and the wind turned icy did she finally look up at me, the night's stars—real ones, not the fake—reflected in her eyes as she nodded and said, "I'd like to go in now."

So I took her hand, leading her all the way back

to my room, and made sure I locked the door behind us.

CHAPTER 6

B ONNIE

Nash's room looked as utilitarian as mine, though he'd likely occupied it for a far shorter time. Both our rooms appeared the same way: like no one lived here beyond the outward shell of us. My fingers trailed the basic bench bolted to the side of the wall, the matching TV that sat in my room.

A mirror image in all things, except for the box he kicked back under his bed the moment he flicked on the lights.

"Your father isn't gonna come in here and bitch slap me for stealing you away?" Nash muttered.

His back turned to me as he tidied the few

personal belongings scattered across one small coffee table, reshuffling a laptop, a spare belt, some chargers.

Nothing I could use to work out who he'd become other than what I'd seen of the man himself.

He turned back to me, his fingers working the next button on his shirt, though he stalled when his gaze coasted along my body to reach my face. "Bonnie?"

I didn't realize I'd started to retreat until my butt bumped the opposite wall of the suddenly cramped room. "I haven't—"

He was across the room, standing in front of me, his hands flexing on my waist before I managed to expel my next breath.

"We don't have to do anything," he promised me, his words at odds with the need that strained his voice, reflecting in the darkest corners of his eyes as he tried to shut the emotion away, and failed.

"I said I would," I started, but he cut me off a second time.

"No. No way am I pushing a girl who says she wants something and then changes her mind. No chance. Especially not you." Nash's touch softened as he pulled me a little closer, still caging me in with his body, though his hold became less threatening. "Nothing you don't wanna do, Bonnie. Everything is your choice." His voice roughened, but he held my gaze with that same formidable, inner strength he'd had even as a wayward teen.

Not that Nash Mercer ever had a rebellious streak, exactly, more the exact opposite. Nothing ever got past him, much as right now.

"I understand," I whispered.

He nodded and lowered his mouth to brush mine in the lightest of kisses, giving me plenty of time to back away. "You want me to take you back to your room now?" His gaze stayed fixed steady on mine.

Whatever he felt inside, he showed nothing on the outside. Maybe that was part of whatever job he took on. At least we'd stopped lying to each other, if only for now.

"Not yet." My fingers twitched at my sides. Before I could question my own motives I buried them in his shirt, digging my fingers into his stomach in a way I was certain couldn't be comfortable. "I just froze up."

"Freezing up is fine." His thumbs skated over my ribs, through the thin material of my dress, beneath my borrowed jacket that still smelled like him.

Whiskey and sea salt and Texas sunshine all at once. A terrible and beautiful dichotomy of all the things I loved and hated that left me homesick for a place I could barely remember. "Wanna watch something old? I have no idea what the resort has on streaming services." He backed off a step, or tried to, but my hands tangled in his shirt, stopping him. The corners of his mouth hooked up when I said nothing, and I didn't move an inch. "Gotta let go, Bonnie, or I'm gonna get the wrong idea."

I tugged at his shirt that loosened from his jeans, and found skin beneath. "So get the wrong idea." I had no idea where the daring words came from, but with Nash, even with that layer of hardness beneath that hadn't ever been there before, he was *safe*.

Safe, in a dangerous kind of way. The sort of man my father kept me away from for all these years under the guise of protecting me when really he just made a cage for a girl who wasn't seventeen wearing ripped jeans and getting a cop to drive her past the prom she couldn't attend any more, but wishing she was still intact like everyone else there that night.

His hands rose along my ribs, traced my upper arms and cupped my jaw. "Be sure, Bonnie. I'll stop any time, but you gotta tell me, okay?" he checked, staring straight through me, into me.

I nodded, licking my lips. "Okay." He said nothing, waited. "Okay, I'll tell you if I need you to stop or I feel...anything."

That mouth I needed on mine moved again. "Good girl."

Then he finally kissed me, his lips crashing sweetly into mine, and no matter what I promised there was no chance I'd be able to tell him anything at all because I never wanted that kiss to end.

So maybe I was still that seventeen year old girl at heart after all, at least a fragment of her, but only in this room, tonight, and only with this man.

No one else, not ever.

Just tonight.

Nash groaned softly as his arms folded tight around me, tucking me into his body. He fit perfectly against me, *still*. Even as a gangly teen he'd been the right size. Never too big, never so overpowering or overprotective that I felt like I'd disappear and never be seen again, overwhelmed by the sheer mass of him.

Even when he kissed me on the beach and engulfed me before, I knew it was only temporary. Nash never stole my identity, took any part of me away from myself. That's what our trust was based on. That, and we *fit* together. Just enough that I knew he could wrap himself around me, hold me up if he wanted.

That sort of strength, along with every other part of him, was sexy as hell. His stomach contracted beneath my fingers as I rediscovered the flat planes of muscle there as well as some scars that hadn't been present before. The landscape of him might have changed over the years, but the way he kissed me, hesitant in hurting me or pushing too hard, too fast, but wanting to go that step further, both of us— that had always been the same.

The difference was that after all this time, I was ready. Truth be told, I'd been ready then. It just took a catastrophic life event for the child in me to be stripped away to recognize that.

But that same girl had a chance to reclaim something tonight.

Nash's kisses grew rougher as he pushed his tongue between my lips, searching for a deeper touch. I arched against him, desperate for the same intimacy, fumbling his buttons with an unsteady hand. My breath shattered against his lips as he laughed softly, a dangerous sound as he scooped me off my feet and lifted me over his bed, yanking back the covers with one arm.

The lights flicked off, leaving us half lit by the

giant Christmas tree's ambient glow outside his window. It was plenty enough to see by, and the warm light left me able to hide, better than the bright down lights.

"Is this okay?" Nash slid his hands under my jacket, pushing both it and the straps of my dress off my shoulders.

My throat worked on nothing at all, and I managed a nod.

"Words, Bonnie." His voice whipped out at me like a slap. I recoiled on the bed, scooting back but he arced over me, boxing me in with his forearms planted beside my head, spreading my legs with his knees. Suddenly, the bed seemed like a threat of its own. "Give me those words you promised, Little Bonnie, or we're going to have a problem." His mouth dipped to trace a line along my collar bone, removing the possibility of speech.

I fell back to the pillows beneath my head, collapsing into a nest made of the scent of him and his scrunched jacket as his weight settled over me. His body pressed into all the right places as I hooked a heel behind his knee, kicking off my shoes.

"I like that," I whispered as he licked and kissed along the hollow of my throat that seemed intent on creating noses of its own.

"I remember." Nash ran a hand down my body to settle at my hip, tugging my dress to my waist. "You know the one fantasy I've had for years that we never played out? Taking you out to the bleachers at the sports field on a sunny afternoon when no one was there, laying you back all bare—" He brushed his palm beneath my dress to discover my silky thong and made a growling sound in his chest, "—take these off, and lick you until you creamed all over my tongue. Then fill you and love you in the sunlight with no one around. Just us. Find out what it felt like to sink into you while you moaned for me, all hot and wet and dirty." He stared down at me, his eyes black and fathomless.

My traitorous body throbbed and clenched on nothing as he cupped my pussy over my panties. "That's a good fantasy," I managed.

His fingertips pressed right over my entrance, no doubt feeling the heat emanating from me at his filthy words that were beyond a turn on because I could imagine him doing exactly what he described just fine. It was the place we shared our first kiss, and even that turned a little X-rated by accident. He'd been a gentleman then, but then heat in his eyes both scared me in all the right ways and turned me on then, too.

So long ago.

But not so long, after all.

"You like that, huh?" Nash pressed in, rubbing my satin panties over my wet pussy.

Swallowing hard, I met the challenge in his eyes. "Show me what you'd do if we were there now," I begged. "Please, Nash. Take me back there tonight."

"Fuck, I love that mouth on you." He bent down and kissed me hard until my lips throbbed, his tongue invading my mouth until I couldn't breathe for the scent of him overflowing my senses.

Even if this was a one night thing, he was imprinted into my brain, my body—and a whole lot deeper—forever.

Nash ran his fingers along my dress and paused. "I wanna rip this right off you, but getting you back to your room and explaining might be tough," he said in a low, strained voice. "If you want me to show you my party trick, I want you to strip for me, love."

I shivered under his lustful gaze. "I—what?"

His lips curled up sinfully. "Tell me you've never watched a dirty movie before, Bonnie."

My cheeks flamed. "Stop that."

"Right. So." He rolled to one side, rubbing his fingers along my stomach. "I want to see you," he whispered, grazing his mouth against my cheek.

"You're so fucking beautiful. Show me every part of you."

This was so far outside my wheelhouse that we'd left the realm of amusing behind long, long ago. But if this was what he wanted, then the people pleaser in me needed to try. Hell, the Nash pleaser in me wanted to try, as well. But my cheeks still flamed as I pushed myself up into a pretzel, his jacket hanging off one shoulder, my legs tucked beneath me.

"I have no idea how to start," I admitted.

His gaze coasted over me as he hooked one finger into the back of my stolen jacket and tugged gently, forcing my shoulders to roll backward, pushing my breasts forward. My head tipped to one side as I watched him, and his mouth brushed over mine.

"That's a damn good start," he breathed.

I let him tug the jacket free, and raised my hands to the dress straps he started on before, slowly sliding them off my shoulders. His eyes tracked that movement too, hunger edging into them as I reached back and started to undo the back of my dress then stopped. I had no bra beneath, which meant I really had to stand up for this next part.

My mouth dried, but it was a now-or-never type decision. Sliding off the bed, I turned my back to him, barely daring to glance over my shoulder. Nash watched me with lazy but heated eyes, his hands resting on his thighs. I slowly lowered the zip in my dress and let it slide to the floor, leaving me in that white, silky thong.

His sharp inhale told me I didn't screw it up, and managed to hook my thumbs into the side straps, wiggling my feet hip width apart and bent forward at the waist, tugging the elastic down. I barely got the panties past my ass cheeks and didn't have to worry about the rest of the mechanics when his hand came down firmly on the small of my back.

"Don't move," Nash said softly, leaving his hand there, though his other traced the curve of my buttock, then a little lower, finding the first drips of dampness and spreading them around.

A whimper left my lips. He said *don't move*, not *don't make any sounds.* I couldn't help the noises that slipped from out as he played with my wet pussy, discovering the shape of my swollen, slick folds, how I shivered when he traced over them, pressed his long fingers into me.

The moment I cried out when he pushed two fingers deep into me and worked them fast he cursed, his hand on my hip gripped tight, before that touch disappeared. His hand closed lightly around my throat, levering my upward.

"Bonnie, you're gonna have to tell me if I can fuck you like this or you want to be back on the bed right now because damn, love, you are far too tempting like that."

He twisted my head back so I had to look at him. My body jostled sideways, and his hand between us rubbed his erection in long, slow strokes that matched his labored breathing.

A sense of power that I'd done this to him, after so long apart, slammed into me.

"However you want, Nash. Just—go slow for a little bit, okay?" Something in my face must have shown through as he cursed again.

A breath later I was on my back with him above me, my thong discarded with the rest of my clothes, alongside his.

"What–?" I swore I wasn't going to get a full sentence out tonight.

"Love, I promise I'll show you everything. But for your first time with me I want to stretch you gently, okay?" His hand found mine and closed my fingers around his—

Girth. Not length. He was worried about actually hurting me.

"Oh, shit." Not eloquent, but it was all I had right then. "I'm more breakable than I thought."

He laughed down at me gently. "Not the way we'll do this, if you're still okay with it. I promise you've gonna like it. But you held up your end. Now it's my turn to take care of you."

Nash pressed me back into the pillow again. Breath whooshed out of me as he slid down my body and between my legs. Then his mouth settled over my bare skin below where I waxed for the beach because I liked the idea of wearing white dresses and white bikinis, never thinking someone else might see me bare.

"Christ, love," he muttered reverently, licking and nibbling on tender flesh. I found his hair and tugged on the short ends, scraping my nails along his scalp as he groaned into my damp skin. "This night is gonna make my top two."

He latched onto my clit at the same time as his tongue dived into my core and I screamed into my fist.

"Oh, God. What was the first?" I panted.

He paused and looked up at me, his brow furrowed. "You don't know?" I shook my head. "Naughty Bonnie," he reproved me in a low voice. "We can deal with that later. The top night is when you got drunk and told me you loved me over a text message back in the day. Best fucking night of my life."

My eyes filled with tears. I tried to answer him, but nothing at all came out. He didn't seem to mind, only went back to the task he set himself, licking and eating me until my legs shook, and he hooked my thighs over his shoulders.

I screamed a second time into my hands, clasping them over my mouth, my heels drumming into his back. Tears cascaded from the corners of my eyes as I came hard.

And the whole time, he never took his eyes off me.

His mouth full of the taste of me—I knew because he climbed up my body, kissing me long and sweet afterward as he rolled on a condom one handed—Nash pressed his thick length at my entrance and pushed in. My fear evaporated by then, and I wound myself around him, my body and heart welcoming the man who held me together over an entire decade, showing me pleasure and pain, adoration after emptiness.

He started slow, but Nash never did anything sweet, not all the way. That edge of danger was always present, always there with him. Once he knew I was alright, his hips slammed into mine as he claimed me over and over. I kissed him back between the noises he bred from me, finding how our bodies and souls fit together after all that time.

This time when I screamed, it was his name into his chest as he cradled me tight to him. I licked the salt of him away as I came down, but he wasn't done. Determination lit his darkened eyes as he marked me inside and out as his. I clung to him and rode the overdose of pleasure out, my mind a splintered mess only holding on enough to hear what he whispered, his lips pressed to my sweat-slicked skin before he roared my name over me, his grip as possessive as his last kisses as the sun rose and the fairytale shattered.

Three words I would cling to no matter what came next for both of us.

"I love you."

Still.

CHAPTER 7

N ASH

We both knew she couldn't stay. Bonnie dozed beside me, one eye on the cheap bedside clock that went off the first night I stayed in the resort at the wrong hour that someone who stayed in the room before me set for some ungodly time and forgot to change before they left.

I promptly reset the thing and forgot about it. Now, I hoped the damn thing failed and never went off ever again.

Bonnie shifted, rolling to face me. "I can feel you watching me," she murmured with her eyes closed.

I trailed my hand along her waist, over the curve

of her hips, though she was so slight, there was barely anything of her. I swore I'd change that, at least a little. What her father did to her...he might try to protect the women in his life, but in his desperation he'd become selfish and cruel.

But that wasn't her worry right now.

"So beautiful." I leaned down and captured her mouth with mine, kissing her long and slow, savoring the sweet taste of her. All stunning and innocent, no matter what she seemed to think.

Years too late, I got the second chance with her I needed, always craved, and never expected to earn. Bonnie sighed beneath me as I pulled her in closer, discarding the notion of time or her father, or her watchdogs. Fuck them all. Right now she was mine, and I refused to give her up.

"Happy Christmas Eve," I murmured against her mouth.

"Is it?" She stared up at me, confusion creasing fine lines around her eyes.

Somehow that made her more beautiful. I wanted all the years with her we missed in between and swore to her and myself silently in my head I'd find a way to make it work for us. Now I had her in my arms again, there was no way I'd let her go. Bonnie Little was the best Christmas present I'd ever had. If I had my way, she'd be Bonnie Mercer come the new year.

If she let me. But by the way her lips twisted prettily as her mind caught up said she wouldn't push me away. At least, not right now. Neither of us put on clothes after I fucked her into the mattress earlier. What started slow blew out fairly fast, which meant I owed my girl an apology.

But when I pressed her onto her back, settling my weight over her, Bonnie's hands shoved lightly at my chest. I backed up in a hurry, and it was my turn to frown. "Did I hurt you? Scare you?" I checked in, cupping her face, pressing my thumb over her pulse point, but her rhythm remained steady, and slow.

"Nope." She popped the 'p' softly, shaking her head and pushed on my chest again. "Off." When I still didn't move, staring down at her intently, she clicked her tongue, the only sign of impatience she offered. "Nash? You got your fantasy time in. Now it's my turn."

Finally, a smile spread over my lips. "You got it." I kissed her again as I peeled my body from hers, barely able to keep my mouth off her, sliding my tongue along hers.

She moaned as she let me roll us, settling her body over mine, her thighs spread to straddle either side of me. When I opened my eyes she sat over me, her dripping pussy rubbing gently over my cock that knew her heat like its own. I caught her hips, but she swatted my hands away, her eyes glowing.

"No, I want to do this myself."

Swallowing back my need to control each grind of her hips along my stiffening length, I tucked my hands behind my head, lacing my fingers together with a supreme effort of willpower. "I'm all yours, love. Anything you want to do."

"Anything, huh?" Bonnie rocked gently against me, slicking me with our mixed fluids, and earning herself a groan from my lips. I couldn't hold back if I wanted to, and there was nothing I wanted to hide from this girl.

The way she looked at me made me wonder if I hadn't just thrown myself in the deep end, but how much trouble could an almost-virginal, twenty-something cloistered ex-girlfriend be?

The moment she slithered along my body, gliding those kiss-bitten lips over my cock and licked my balls, I knew I was screwed. Or about to be.

I should have studied the ceiling. The light fixtures. An errant, missed cobweb.

Instead, I watched her lashes sweep over her blush-stained cheeks as she explored me like we never got to do back then. Before our worlds were thrown into a maelstrom of uncertainty and separate hells.

My breath shuddered from my lungs as I scratched vicious patterns into my scalp where she couldn't see, desperate to wrap my hands in her hair and fuck her pretty little mouth until she sobbed and choked for me. But I promised I'd let her have her way, and I was a man of my word.

For now.

Bonnie graduated from exploring my thighs and everything below my cock with her tongue and hit the main event, fitting as much of me in her mouth with one swallow as she could.

I swore I drew blood on the back of my neck. A long hiss burst from my lips as my legs stiffened.

She broke her concentration, looking up at me, her mouth stuffed full of cock, lashes obscuring her eyes as her tongue flicked over my cock head. My balls drew up painfully tight as I willed myself not to paint her tongue with my seed, desperate to feel her sink down on me once she finished torturing me.

Finally she released me, her lips pinched. "Am I doing it wrong?"

I released my hands from behind my head,

relieved to see no blood caked beneath my nails, and crooked a finger. "Come here," I ordered softly.

She crawled up my body, hovering over me. Her hair draped across my shoulders, tight nipples grazing my pecs. "Tell me what I did?" she begged prettily.

I caught her chin in a firm grip. "What you did was nearly make me come in your mouth, love," I admitted, freeing up my other hand to swat her ass.

She squealed in a delayed reaction. "Nash," she gasped a breath later, clawing my shoulders.

I smirked. "What, daddy never smacked his princess?"

Her gaze lowered. "You know he didn't."

I found her glorious tits and toyed with them until she panted, twirling the nipples between forefinger and thumb and tugging her closer. "That's alright, Bonnie. I'll pick up what's been left out. Make sure you're looked after. You need another?"

I pinched her nipple slowly, not too hard, but hard enough. Letting her feel the pain develop, I kept a hold until a second after my name left her lips again.

Hesitant, she met my eyes again and nodded, just once.

I urged her closer and tucked her into my body, sweeping my hand over her ass where I spanked her before. When she breathed out, I planted my palm in the same spot, a little softer on her already warmed flesh. She didn't jolt as much this time, but her heat increased over my groin.

"Say thank you," I murmured against her cheek, tasting the dampness of her tears. "It's okay if you need to let it out. You've been living a fucked up little life, love. Anything you need, I promise I'll give it to you."

"Thank you, Nash. Maybe, just one more? The other side. Please," she added belatedly.

"My pleasure." I kissed her sweetly for begging so well, sliding my tongue along hers, then drew back to watch her face as I spanked her hard on the other side.

A single tear trickled down her cheek as she trembled for me and let out the most beautiful, relaxed sigh.

I swept the salty drop back with my thumb, pressing her tear to the corner of her lips. "Taste, Bonnie. That's your freedom. What you take," I reminded her. "Every step you get is for yourself. Can you breathe?"

I held her close, wanting to roll us both and slide inside her, but I promised her, and dammit that oath was gonna kill me.

"Yes," she whispered. "It's not so impossible now."

"God, you're fucking beautiful." I kissed her again, arranging her how she was when she started. "You said you had a fantasy. I can take over if you need. Whatever you want, Bonnie."

Her hands played with my stomach, tracing over the scars there, some of the old knife and bullet wounds I earned in service. Some cops went years without drawing a weapon. I put myself in the line of fire the moment I earned my badge because I couldn't sleep at night if I drove a desk all damn day. Lost thinking about her, never allowed to investigate her case.

Until now.

And all I wanted to do was take her away from it all, throw my career away and run with her somewhere nothing else mattered but her freedom.

Fuck it, after Christmas I might do it anyway. The whole vengeance thing no longer mattered anywhere near as much as it did when I arrived at Love Beach. The box of files under my bed burned a hole in my back as she straddled me, some of her confidence regained with her glowing behind.

Bonnie let me grip her hips this time, helping guide her as she caught my cock in her hand and raised herself over me, then slid down my length, her heat enveloping me until we both moaned, entangled in each other's arms.

And I forgot everything except for the soft girl wrapped around me, her breasts pressed to my chest, her heart beating too fast with mine. Bonnie worked out how to ride me while I tried my damn-dest not to coat her walls with the pleasure of being bare inside her. Too late the thought ran through my head, but the moment I tried to shift, she shook her head, recognition crossing her face.

"Implant," she whispered.

I swallowed hard, finding her ass cheeks I spanked before and bottoming out in her in one go as I levered myself up to press my back to the bed's headboard. "I'm clean, love. Are you sure?" I searched her face. "I know I promised, but I'm not a god. And you feel so fucking good I just want to rail you into the bed until my name is the only thing on your lips."

Bonnie's lips parted a fraction, her breath kissing my cheeks. "Do it," she whispered.

We never go that far.

I slammed her down onto my cock, her ass a two-handed grip as I pounded into her swollen, needy pussy from below. Over and over, until she cried my name on repeat into my ear. The soundtrack I came to, my neck straining, still not letting her go as I fused our bodies together and filled her to the brim.

My orgasm hurt like a fucking truck smashing into me, ripping my insides out, the lines of pleasure and pain melding. The only thing I felt after was her heat wrapped around me, her body trembling after the way I railed her. And finally my senses came back to me.

"Christ, tell me I didn't actually hurt you," I muttered, pushing her hair aside until I found her face tucked into my shoulder in a pool of sweat and saliva. "Bonnie. Love?" I cupped her chin and tilted her head up to mine.

Her makeup smeared beneath her eyes, her cheeks stained a violent red as she panted gently.

"I'm good," she whispered. "Just...wow. Are you like that all the time?"

I laughed, resting back against the wall, half expecting the bed to collapse beneath us both at any moment. "Just with you, love. Only you."

I stroked her hair, tucking her back where I excavated her from and managed a breath. The time, the clock, the world was all forgotten as we came down from the incredible high of falling into each other again and finding out we got it right the first time around.

CHAPTER 8

N ASH

When the threat came, I had all the timings wrong. Bonnie and I managed to spend the morning in each other's arms without incident until the door to my room was kicked in without any prior announcement.

"That's just fucking rude," I muttered as I rubbed sleep from my eyes with one hand and tucked her beneath the blankets with the other, figuring her father would at least knock.

That was the part I got wrong. Not the knocking, her father.

Because I found myself looking down the wrong

end of a gun no one ever wanted to be on, and I'd had enough of that particular end for a lifetime.

"Fuck me." I pushed Bonnie behind me as I stared at a man I didn't know who hadn't bothered to cover his face, and that fact alone boded really shittily for the start of Christmas Eve for both of us right when I found the first spark of happiness in a long damn time.

The second part of it was that while his gun was pointed at me, his attention was on *her*.

"Get out," he snapped, as though he expected her to know him. "I'll deal with you shortly."

I couldn't risk taking my eyes off him, but the way Bonnie stiffened behind me, then shifted away, told me I miscalculated really fucking badly.

"Love, I need you to use those words you promised me before," I murmured, gliding my hand under my pillow for the gun that should have been there, but wasn't.

Where the fuck is it?

"I'm sorry, Nash," she replied, her voice way too steady for my liking. A metaphorical sucker punch hit me in the back, right in the damn kidneys, and stole all my air.

"Sorry for...? Give me something more," I muttered, more than a little desperate.

"Sorry for this." Sadness filled her voice, enough that I risked turning to look at her.

In time to see her raise the handgun I was missing, flick the safety expertly off and double tap the asshole holding the gun on us.

The fact he never fired before he fell, never made a single sound, told me he expected the move less than I did.

I didn't turn around to check. She hadn't missed, not at that range, not with that confidence or skill level. My cock stirred at the image of her burned forever into my mind holding that gun, naked, her legs spread apart, fierce determination written across her stunning face even as my eardrums protested at the noise abuse.

"Damn, girl. If this is how I die, I'm good with it," I breathed when my head stopped ringing.

She managed a hiccup as she lowered my gun. I caught her as her knees bent, collapsing beneath her. The gun tumbled from her hand. I caught that too, flicking the safety back on, and sliding it beside the box under the bed. Then I tucked her into my side and wrapped the blankets around her as she began to shake, her brief spurt of adrenaline leaving her as fast as it came on.

"Never actually taken out a live target before,

huh?" I kissed the top of her head. "Proud of you, love."

She hiccupped amongst the sobs. "You have?"

"Yeah." I huffed out a laugh. "Couple of times now. Still feel shit on the inside no matter what I pretend. Wanna tell me who taught you to shoot like that?"

"I did."

The knock I expected still didn't come, but with the door kicked in like that, who needed to knock?

Grant Little-Lawson stared back at me when I turned my head, then his attention dropped to the body on the floor. "I'm sorry it had to be you."

I figured he wasn't talking to me, or the dead man staining the carpet. "Someone gonna tell me why I got a dead body on the floor and why I have to explain to my boss why my gun was fired by someone who isn't me?" I didn't let go of Bonnie, and she still shook in my arms beneath the sheets.

Grant made the wise choice not to comment on the fact that we shared a bed, nor our state of undress. He did, however, need to start talking, or she did, because resort management and the local cops were going to be up our combined asses in a matter of minutes.

As much as I enjoyed being a Texas Ranger, that

shiny little star didn't mean shit halfway across the country. For the first time since I resigned, I missed my FBI badge with a vengeance.

"I want to tell him."

Bonnie's voice came from the region of my armpit. I tugged gently on her hair and ignored her father who didn't scare me half as much as he had when I was a kid.

"Love, if you want to tell me your story then you'd better hurry up. We have a very limited time before I'm going to need to explain myself and put pants on." I paused. "And we should probably move to a different room." The small living area off my bedroom would do. While I was used to the aroma of death, I doubted Bonnie had that life experience.

Grant sighed. "I'll run interference. Buy you a few minutes. Best talk fast, Bon-Bon."

I carried Bonnie to the two-seater sofa, still wrapped in the sheet, collecting our clothes as we went.

Her fingers flicked at my side, nails scratching my ribs lightly at the nickname she never told him she hated. "I'll be quick," she muttered, tickling me with her breath.

I waited until Grant left the apartment, positioning his bulk with his back to the doorway so no one could see in, and hauled her out of my tickle zone to slam my mouth down on hers. "That was the sexiest fucking thing I've ever seen, love," I murmured into her mouth.

Grant coughed not so discreetly from the resort room doorway.

Bonnie grimaced, ignoring both him and the dead man congealing on the floor behind us, but at least we didn't have to breathe him in now.

"I need clothes," she whispered.

My arms wrapped around her middle as I hauled her against me. "Right now you need to tell me what the fuck happened." I captured her jaw between my fingers and fixed her with a hard stare. "I'm not gonna leave you to face any of this alone. I'm not leaving *you*, love. But I need information, because I can't protect you without that."

Her mouth made the sweetest little moue without her knowing it, I thought, and I kissed her before she could say anything. Hands swatted at my shoulders until I gave her air.

"I can't talk if you do that," she hissed. "I–"

Her gaze darted to the door, and my arms tightened. Breath left her, and it was like her entire body deflated. I knew she wasn't ready to talk but we'd run out of the luxury of time. Her heart rate picked up against my arms as I pressed my lips to her temple and promised I'd make love to her at some future point.

Sometime. When I could contain myself from needing to screw us both into next week. Month.

Year.

With my name next to hers on a certificate.

"The night you were supposed to take me—" she stalled. I gave her time, stroking her arms and tried not to glance back at the doorway, counting mentally in my head and ignoring the stupid damn clock. "That night you, we— everyone. Daddy had people around while I got ready. Men." Her voice cracked.

My arms tightened about her frame. I loosened them with effort. "It's okay, love. I won't leave you, and they can't hurt you now. Looks like your daddy taught you how to protect yourself just fine."

After the fact, maybe, but Grant went up a notch in my estimation.

I leaned back, grabbing for our clothes I collected earlier, and dressed her one-handed as she talked, then myself.

"They came into my room. After their meeting. Something about the school, wanting to limit who attended. Daddy, he didn't like it."

"Bonnie." I kissed her temple. My eyes weren't

the only ones on the door. I had a damn good idea where this conversation was headed.

Her tears drenched my arm long before she told me what she kept inside all these years. "I couldn't stop them. Too many. My dress was ripped."

I swallowed. She went shopping for that damn dress with her mother weeks before prom. I remembered I hadn't been allowed to see it. They teased me with the thought of her dressed up and I played along, aching to see her, waiting for her. So damn gorgeous just in jeans and a t-shirt. My girl.

"Fuck, Bonnie." I kissed her mouth before she could keep talking. "Love you."

"Love you, too."

The platitude didn't go far, but she pressed into me as I fixed the back of her dress and managed to wrap my belt around my waist, checking for my wallet, my badge I'd need the moment the local cops rocked up, and a different sort of rock.

"Mom came in halfway through. She saw everything." Bonnie's voice broke in full. "He held down, and she tried to help but they'd, I don't know, someone kept Daddy away. He didn't know, couldn't help. He was heartbroken after. Called the police, reported everything. But they police were—"

She choked, and I filled in the rest of the story

because I knew this one by heart. Coldness filled my veins.

"The police were paid off because he owned them, didn't he?" I recited by rote. "My grandfather." Fuck. The one case I'd been after, all these years. If I'd been able to put him away earlier, she'd have been free that much sooner. "This was his man, wasn't he?" I jerked my head back toward the body cooling on the carpet. She nodded, and sucked in a breath. "The reason you haven't been able to come back to Texas at all?" Another nod. "Christ, love. I've failed you. Not being there for you."

"I wasn't allowed to. The police. I– they took me away. I– I asked them to drive past the prom. I saw you that night. You looked so angry."

I stared down at her, horror building in my gut. "I saw that. The police car. I thought it was a routine drive by, checking on the kids. Our safety." I uttered a hollow laugh. You were right fucking there, love. I could have–" I slammed a fist backward into the plaster by the headboard and put my knuckles right through the wall.

Bonnie didn't even flinch, only burrowed deeper into my chest, her tears soaking my shirt, but I didn't care. Her hand slipped through my fingers, trying to pry my hand open, kissing the tiny cuts I put on my own skin.

"Don't hurt yourself. Nash, please, let me hold your hand–"

Her desperate plea snapped off as I opened my fingers, displaying the diamond ring sitting in the middle of my palm.

"I've had this in my pocket ever since that night. I knew it was too early, and it was everything I had saved for a car we talked about me buying that I used on this instead." I caught her hand and as she nodded, her lips parted, I slipped the ring always meant for her onto her finger. Her tears flowed fresh and fast as I kissed her knuckles, folding my bloodied ones over hers. "I love you, Bonnie. I want my name next to yours forever. It's always been us." I searched her eyes. "I wish I'd been there. Would have fought for you. But damn, girl. I'll fight for you now." I hit stop on the recording on my phone, knowing I'd need that later, and pulled her in for a deep kiss when she didn't fight me.

She nodded, but her eyes were serious when I let her breathe. "What if I'm in jail for the next twenty years for killing a man?"

"That? That was defense, love. I promise." I sent

off two messages, one to my local FBI contact, the next to Archer, and pocketed my phone.

That pocket suddenly seemed a hell of a lot lighter. "Wanna tell your daddy before the cops arrive and we gotta tell them everything all over again?"

She kept on nodding, and let me lead her back around the dead man whose name I still didn't know to Grant.

He didn't turn his head when she hugged him, but did hold out an arm. "I heard," he said gruffly. "You sure you want to be hitched to a Texas Ranger, Bon-Bon?"

She glanced at me with wide eyes. "Is that what you are?"

I shrugged. "It's new to me, too. I was FBI."

"Oh." She blinked at me. "Daddy? We're getting married in Texas."

He looked down at her and ignored me. "You trust him?"

"We always should have."

My heart glowed in my chest as she released her father and slipped her arms around my waist.

Then, we waited.

EPILOGUE

BONNIE

Three days after Christmas, most of which we spent in a very prettily decorated police station at Love Beach, Nash drove us across the country back to Texas. I stood at the border of the land I last saw a decade and change ago, wondering if I was actually allowed to step foot onto my native home.

Mom and Dad were taking their time coming back, and I didn't think it was all about Mom, though Dad insisted it was. Part of me wondered how much he didn't want to see Texas again, either. Nash offered his own home open to us while we found our feet again, and his Texas Rangers provided protection for my entire family, and me.

It was like they adopted us the moment his case blew open, though I knew he hadn't been part of them for very long either. A new family for all. Merry Christmas, bordering on a new year.

Even a happy one.

Part of me still struggled with the fact I killed a man, thanks to Daddy teaching me years ago how to handle a gun until the guise of taking me hunting as a kid and swapping out my rifle on occasion for a handgun I suspected he stole from somewhere.

That was back in the early days when he seemed to think we might escape from our hideous life moving from place to place under the watchful eye of Texas' worst and most dreadful.

They didn't seem to want to pull the trigger on our strange impasse, and we ended up in an endless bout of self-inflicted purgatory. I think they were waiting for us to implode, but that never happened thanks to Daddy's deep, deep pockets.

Now, that long, stagnant stage of my life was over. A full third, and I was free thanks to Nash's quick talking to the local police and his connections with law enforcement.

Which brought us, quite literally, back to Texas.

"Bonnie," Nash said my name like a caress. He stood with his hand outstretched, him on the other side of that state line. After this we'd still have a long way to go to get to his home, but right here, this moment—it meant so much to both of us.

My heart lived on that land, with him. But my feet flat out refused to move.

"How did you do it?" I pleaded, locking my fingers together into a knot. "When you were called back."

Nash considered me for a long moment before he answered. "I wanted answers. I wanted that case to close up with my grandfather. My mother hadn't seen me in years, and I didn't call because I pushed her and everyone else away." He took a step closer until we were toe to toe with an invisible line dividing us, a breath wide. "But most of all, I wanted to find you."

My eyes shuttered, tears dropping with them. One day I'd stop crying, but today the tears still fell. One day. Maybe.

I reached out and he lifted me off my feet, turning us in a circle and placed me on Texas land.

My feet didn't move. Heat ran up my ankles, but the ground didn't shake, and the world didn't end.

"How does it feel to be home, love?"

I smiled into his shirt, breathed in his leather and whiskey and caramel scent, ran my fingers over the star badge he displayed on his belt, and smiled.

"Like I'm supposed to be here with you."

Read more Nash and Bonnie

(and that bleacher fantasy he detailed back at the resort)

in their BONUS EPILOGUE FOR FREE

Thank you for reading MERRY WITH A RANGER! Nash and Bonnie's story turned out to have a hugely more emotional punch than I expected (hey, it happens!) and thank you so much for sticking with us to the end. Please do leave a review. I appreciate and read every single one.

What to read next:

Check out MERRY WITH A BREWMASTER and continue the fun at Love Beach through the holidays.

Be sure to check out the rest of the books in the Multi-Author Love Beach Collection. Also, the Love Beach Authors invite you to join us for more fun including free eBooks, giveaways, cocktail recipes, and more on the Love Beach Fan Page.

Following on with TEXAN DEVILS after Nash...

SUMMER WITH A RANGER (HUDSON)
   Snapdragons & Seductions (Acton)

TEXAN DEVILS
   RANGER'S WISH
   RANGER BEDEVILLED
   RANGER'S PASSION
   RANGER'S FURY
   RANGER'S WRATH
   RANGER'S DILEMMA
   RANGER'S STORM

RED HART RANCH (crossover series)
   SNOW ON THE RANGE
   SIREN ON THE RANGE
   SUNDOWN ON THE RANGE
   SHADOW ON THE RANGE
   SPIRIT ON THE RANGE

ABOUT THE AUTHOR

USA Today Bestselling author Sofia Aves writes fast-paced police romances, sizzling military units, steamy cowboys with a Montana backdrop and the occasional cheeky god. Married to a veteran, she often tackles topics of PTSD and reintegration and has a soft spot for all who work in uniform. Sofia writes kidlit for charity and has over one hundred and fifty publications across four not-so-super-secret pen names.

Publishing is her life. She has been a marketing manager for both Romance Writers of Australia, and Romance Cafe Publishing and an acquisitions editor for Evernight and Evernight Teen. Sofia is a mum of three crazies in a returned veteran household and has an overly large fur baby who thinks she's a teacup puppy. After eighteen years of planning and dreaming, Sofia and her husband will put the finishing touches on their very own alpaca park this year. Sofia lives near Brisbane, Australia.

Read Sofia's Series

Rippton Allstars

Blue Blooded Brothers

Red Hart Ranch

Texan Devils

Z Boys

Writing spicy paranormal romance as RAVEN HUSH

Club Fray

Monster Brides

Silent Sentinels